Wish Kitten

Written and Illustrated by Grace Marshall

Grace D. Marshall

A special thanks to Ms. Bartlett and Mr. Pullan, two teachers
who helped me through the whole process and always believed in me,
as well as my parents who patiently listened to my many drafts.

"For greed, all nature is too little" - Seneca

1

The Warner Family didn't believe in magic, witchcraft, or wishes coming true. They were a very logical family, and nothing out of the ordinary ever happened to them in their large, grey house with neatly trimmed hedges and a chimney in the middle on 21 Lordewood Lane. That is why it was a surprise when Willow Warner, the younger of the two Warner children, opened the big red entry door one cold and dreary day to find a little kitten perched on the edge of the welcome mat, staring up at her. He was a nice-looking tabby kitten, with his sleek brown and white fur and perfectly point-ed ears, except that his eyes were completely clouded over, as if he was blind. Willow thought this was indeed the reason for his strangely colored eyes, and she crouched down to say hello to the little thing. It didn't take long for small Willow to realize how fun and wonderful this kitten was, and just how much she dearly wanted to keep him.

Now, Willow was a practical individual--like her parents and older brother--and knew that it would be very illogical to keep a kitten in a house where no pets had ever set foot and think that her parents would have nothing to say in the matter. But she also knew that she couldn't leave the kitten out in the cold, so she brought him inside and showed him to her parents. Mr. and Mrs. Warner didn't think it very wise, yet the pleading look on their daughter's face was something that they hadn't seen her wear in a long time, for rare was the occasion that either of the Warner children begged. So they gave in. Little Willow was so pleased that she didn't even notice the kitten was smiling.

2

On the fourth night of the kitten's stay, Willow awoke to a noise coming from downstairs. It was faint, but the youngest member of the Warner Family had exceptionally good hearing, and she woke from her sleep almost instantly. Sneaking from her room, she tiptoed past her older brother William's door and crept down the stairs. The noise was louder now, and Willow realized that it was someone singing. The only plausible explanation was that someone had left the television or radio on, but Willow knew that her father and mother were very organized and would never leave on any of their electronics without realizing that they had. Besides, they only listened to the news, and singing was certainly not part of the news. Sneaking up to the doorway which led to the dimly lit living room, Willow stepped into the doorframe and paused. In the corner by the turquoise couch, where they had made up a bed for him out of a cardboard box and an old pillow, the little creature sat facing towards the wall. Willow knew that she had to be dreaming, but didn't know why it seemed so real. Listening closer, she heard the soft lyrics to the song:

Wish Kitten, Wish Kitten, grant me a wish, fix all my problems, as quick as a fish.
Wish Kitten, Wish Kitten, I'll do it for you, if you just do what I tell you to do.

Willow didn't know what to make of it except that she was having quite an odd dream and wondered if the kitten in the dream was singing to her or to himself. But before she could think of anything else, the kitten stopped singing and said (yes, indeed, said, because the words were coming from the kitten's mouth although he was still turned around), "Little girl, what are you doing up so late?"

Willow decided to answer, for it was only a dream after all, and she would be awake soon anyway. "I heard you singing." She said, quietly.

The kitten turned his head almost all the way around. It reminded Willow of an owl with whiskers. Two clouded white eyes stared up at her. "You have sharp ears, little girl."

Willow nodded and took a step into the living room. It wouldn't hurt to get closer, since it was a dream after all. "You can talk."

The kitten smiled, the ends of his mouth reaching up to his whiskers. "Oh, I can do much more than that."

She inched closer and asked, "Like what, kitty?"

He turned the rest of his body so that he was completely facing Willow. "I can grant wishes."

"Wishes?" She sat down in front of him, folding her little hands neatly on her pajama-clad lap to keep from fidgeting with things. Her parents always said that excitement was best not shown through squirming--it wasn't sensible.

"Indeed. Wishes." The kitten's tail wrapped around himself.

"Any kind of wish?" Willow could think of a few that she had hoped would come true for a while now.

"Any kind." He blinked, so quickly that it almost looked as if he hadn't. "Is there something that you would like to wish for, little girl?"

Willow thought for a moment. She really wanted a teddy bear that she had seen in the toy store window downtown, but her mother didn't like stuffed animals, for she thought that they were simply objects designed to pacify babies. In Mrs. Warner's eyes, Willow was no longer a little kid and she thought it ridiculous to indulge such infantile tendencies. Besides, who needed stuffed animals when you had books? Yet Willow secretly wanted the bear more than she let on, because pining in the Warner family was strictly forbidden. But simply asking, on the other hand, was a different story. The small girl said softly, "I wish I could have a teddy bear."

"It will be granted. All you have to do is say please."

"Please?" Willow whispered.

At this, the kitten closed his big white eyes and seemed to stop breathing for a moment. But then, just as quickly, his eyes flashed open and he began purring again. "If you go upstairs, you will find what you seek."

Willow hopped to her feet, and then stopped. "Are you sure it will be there?"

"There's only one way to find out," He smiled, "Goodnight, little Miss Warner."

Willow waved and snuck back up the stairs to her room. There, sitting on her bed, she found a little stuffed teddy bear, propped up at the foot of her bed as if it had been there all along.

3

For the next couple of nights, Willow visited the kitten. Sometimes it was to ask for wishes, sometimes to just talk. She felt that the kitten understood her like no one else in the house did. But one night, William Warner woke up to see his little sister sneaking down the stairs. He slipped out of bed and followed her silently, only to find her walk straight up to the kitten and start talking to it. William watched the kitten respond as if it were a completely normal and logical thing for a kitten to speak. William, of course, gasped at this phenomenon and blew his cover. The kitten looked up at William and said, "Come out, little boy. Your sister was just about to ask me for another wish."

William Warner knew nothing else to do except obey, since no one ever told him whether or not he should do what a kitten says. When William walked over to his sister, she excitedly explained to him how nice the kitten was and how it would grant whatever you wished for if you just said please. William wished, please, for a bright red fire truck. Sure enough, a bright red fire truck was found right next to William's toy box when he went back to bed that night. But one of the things you must know about William Warner is that he was not good at keeping secrets, especially from Mr. and Mrs. Warner. So, after a few nights of creeping downstairs to have wishes granted, William convinced Willow to tell their parents about the wishing kitten with him.

Mr. and Mrs. Warner obviously didn't believe their children, but since they were a very logical couple and they realized that their children had never produced a lie of this size before, the Warner parents decided that they would investigate this so-called "talking" feline. So, following their children's directions, Mr. and Mrs. Warner got up in the dead of night and made their way down to where the kitten slept in the living room. Sure enough, and to their amazement, the kitten politely introduced himself.

He smiled at their astonishment and said, "Oh, don't look so surprised. It's only sensible that a kitten who can grant wishes can also talk."

When the Warner parents were reluctant to ask for a wish, since they didn't trust anything that was free, the kitten assured them that it wasn't completely free--they still had to say please. This seemed to satisfy Mr. and Mrs. Warner enough and, although they thought it silly, they both asked for a wish.

Mr. Warner immediately received a phone call from his boss telling him that he had moved up in his job and Mrs. Warner hurried up to her room to find a brand new fur coat laying neatly on her bed. The Warner couple were blown away by the impossibility of it all, to which the kitten smiled smugly and purred, "I told you. Now why would I lie to such a smart family?"

When they asked the creature how he did it, he responded, "Wishes are tricky things. They are too fast for most to catch, but not for me. I hunt them down and snatch them... Like catching a little bird with a broken wing."

"So, not magic?" Mrs. Warner questioned.

The kitten emitted an eerie cackling sound that was his laugh. "Of course not. Don't you know there's no such thing as magic?"

Mr. and Mrs. Warner didn't quite know how to respond to this. It didn't make a lot of sense, but talking kittens didn't make much sense either, so they accepted it. From that night forward, the Warner family slowly began to change. Once they accepted the impossible, the Warners soon found themselves relying less and less on their logic and reason. This wouldn't have been a problem if the family hadn't built their whole lives upon these ideas. So in order to fill the space which the rationality left, the Warners found themselves relying more and more on the wishes that the kitten granted. Within a week, the family became increasingly wealthier and the house was quickly stocked with bins of new toys for the children, closets of fancy dresses for Mrs. Warner, and a shiny new Chevrolet Bel Air for Mr. Warner. At one point they even created a chart dividing up nights for different people to go and ask for wishes, but greediness got the best of them and the chart was ultimately disregarded. Summer quickly turned to fall and the Warners became almost completely reliant on the kitten's wishes to ful-fill their every desire. Although it was difficult to tell at first, the Warner family began to fall apart.

4

It all came to a head one rainy morning as the Warners scurried around the house getting ready for the day. During the short time that the kitten had stayed there, the big grey house had slowly become unorganized and cluttered with piles of needless items they had wished for--something which would never have happened just a couple of months before. As a result of the mess, things started going missing and turning up in places they shouldn't.

"Mom, where's the cereal this time?" William asked, opening and closing the kitchen cabinet doors loudly in exasperation.

"How am I supposed to know? Ask your father!" Mrs. Warner called from the other room, irritation lacing her voice.

William opened the dishwasher to retrieve a bowl, only to discover a box of wholegrain cereal tucked into the top rack. "Never mind, I found it!" yelled William, pulling the box from its unusual resting place.

Mr. Warner rushed into the kitchen, shirt untucked and a concerned expression etched into his strong features. "Has anyone seen my keys?" He demanded.

Mrs. Warner's annoyed voice could be heard through the open door as she squawked, "Have you checked the freezer?"

Navigating around the mounds of miscellaneous objects that cluttered the kitchen, Mr. Warner opened the freezer door and found his keys on one of the frozen shelves. "Why did you put them in here, Wendy?"

An annoyed Mrs. Warner marched into the kitchen with curlers in her hair and a purple striped robe wrapped around her. "I didn't put them in there! They're *your* keys!"

Her husband turned to face her and replied sharply, "Yes, but *you* drove my car yesterday!"

Anger rose up in Mrs. Warner and her face turned red with rage as she spat, "It's not *my* fault that we only have one car!"

"If you're so anxious to go places then why don't you wish for your own car?!" Mr. Warner countered.

"Fine, I will!"

William, who had been watching the argument unfold in silence, interjected, "But it was my turn to wish for something!"

The littlest Warner then spoke from the corner of the room, where she had been eating a cold bagel. "No, it was my turn, William. You went the time before last."

"Did not!" William protested.

"Did too!" Willow cried.

"Children, stop bickering! It's not becoming of someone to argue all the time." scolded their mother, curlers bouncing as she stepped between the two children.

Mr. Warner turned and muttered under his breath, "Says the woman who can't go a blessed minute without complaining."

But Mrs. Warner had sharp ears whenever she was being talked about, and she snapped, "What did you say?!"

The kitchen burst forth with noise as arguing erupted between the different family members. All of the voices blended into one giant clamor as accusations got thrown around and no one listened to one another. The uproar continued to rise in volume until Mr. Warner roared above all of the other voices, "SILENCE!"

The room instantly hushed at his command and all eyes fixed upon Mr. Warner in shock. He suddenly looked very tired and rubbed the creases from his forehead before asking softly, "What happened to us? Why are we always arguing over the silliest things?"

The rest of the Warner family looked down at the tiled floor in shame as Mr.

Warner continued, "It wasn't that long ago when we were perfectly orderly and happy. Now look at this place!" He gestured at the mess of random items they had wished for and then discarded around the house. "We're a mess. We're a complete mess."

Mrs. Warner stepped forward and lightly placed a hand on her husband's arm, tears welling up in her eyes. "I'm sorry, Wesley. I don't know how it happened." Mr. Warner was silent for a moment and then looked up with a fierceness in his eye that frightened Willow. "I do."

The Warner family glanced at the head of the household in confusion and he stated, "It's the kitten. Ever since he came to this house, he's clouded our minds with wishes and magic to the point where we aren't ourselves anymore... We have to get rid of him."

Both of the Warner children gasped and Willow cried, "No!"
"Sweetie, your father is right," Mrs. Warner gazed down at her daughter with a twinge of sadness. "This is as hard for us as it is for you, but it has to be done... We'll take him to the shelter in the morning."

Although it took a bit of coaxing, William finally came around to the idea of giving away the kitten. Willow, on the other hand, had grown attached to the kitten and didn't like the idea of giving him away one bit. She begged her parents to reconsider, hot tears pouring down her little face and a strong sense of betrayal bubbling up in her. But Mr. and Mrs. Warner simply replied, "It's not good for children to beg. Begging isn't reasonable."

When Willow turned to William for affirmation, her brother just gave her a sad look, as if to say, "Poor little girl; she doesn't know what's good for her." Willow quickly became furious at her family's harshness towards the kitten. Because she had been the one to find it and had talked to it more than all of the other Warners combined, Willow felt that she had established a special bond with the animal; something that she had never had with any of the little boys or girls her age. The kids at her school didn't understand her like the kitten did, and it greatly troubled her that she might lose her only true friend. Hostility towards her family welled up inside Willow and, in a moment of blind rage, she stamped her small foot and yelled, "I hate all of you! I wish... I wish we got rid of you!"

The Warner family gasped at Willow's cutting words. After a second of stunned silence, Mrs. Warner grabbed her daughter by the arm and hissed, "Don't you dare talk to us like that, Willow!"

"That is no way to talk to your parents, young lady!" Mr. Warner scolded, frowning down at his daughter. He had never allowed his children to talk back to him in his house, but it had never been a problem before. Yet he knew what the problem really was; the kitten had gotten into Willow's susceptible brain somehow and there was only one thing to keep it from corrupting all of their minds. "That settles it! Wendy, we're taking the kitten to a shelter right now. Willow, go straight up to your room to think long and hard about what you've said and William, look after your sister while we're gone."

And so, on a cold, dreary day similar to the one which had occurred when Willow first found the creature, the Warner parents dropped the little kitten off at a shelter a few hours away. Once they had gotten home, the family cleared the house of the unnecessary litter and Willow sincerely apologized for her terrible outburst. With order and logic restored, all was finally back to normal in the big grey house on Lordewood Lane. Or at least, so the Warners thought.

15

5

A day after they had taken the kitten to the shelter, the whole family was woken up in the middle of the night by a loud thumping noise coming from the front door. Mr. Warner told his wife and children to stay while he went down to investigate, but Willow and William's curiosity got the best of them and they ran after their father, followed by Mrs. Warner who tried to no avail to get her children to obey her. Once they were all downstairs, the thumping noise turned into frantic scratching sounds on the door. Of course, the logical thing for Mr. or Mrs. Warner would have been to phone the police, but the frantic scratching reminded them of a particular kitten who could grant wishes, and they froze at the thought of it. Something about coming in contact with the impossible struck fear into the Warner parents like nothing had before. And then the big red door slowly unlocked itself.

As the Warner family stood frozen in fear, the door was pushed open to reveal the silhouette of a small kitten with two glowing, unblinking eyes. The shadow took a step forward and said, "All I wanted was a place to stay, but you kicked me out. I caught your wishes and yet your thanks was to get rid of me. Don't worry dear family, I know I am not welcome here anymore, but I have only come back to grant your very last wish."

The kitten stepped into the house and tilted his head to the side slightly. A giant smile suddenly burst onto his face, growing bigger than any of his previous smiles and exposing his rows of long, pointy teeth. In its strange scratchy voice the kitten chanted, "Did you miss me, naughty little birds?"

6

It had been three years since anyone had lived in the large, stately grey house on 21 Lordewood Lane, with its now overgrown hedges and peeling paint. Ever since the family who had previously owned it disappeared suddenly in the middle of the night-- save the smallest child, who was whisked off to an orphanage far away--the house was said to be haunted. It was one of those places that children ran past when going to school, afraid that if they lingered for too long out in front of it then something might come out of the marred front door. It was an ongoing dare in the neighborhood for kids to go up and touch the house, but none of them had ever gone into the house before. Until a particularly brave girl by the name of Penelope Park moved to town.

Penelope was a tomboy who wasn't scared of adventure and had plenty of scars to prove it. She loved showing off her fearlessness, so when the neighboring kids dared her to go and touch the big grey house, she accepted and then shocked them by saying she would even go so far as to walk into it. None of the children believed her until she marched up to the front door of the house, which had massive scratches stretching the length of it, and yanked it open. All of the kids stood in awe as she disappeared into the house without even hesitating.

Once inside the house, Penelope was surprised at how neat it was. Except for the dust that covered everything, it looked like a completely normal home. Penelope walked across the checkered floors and carpeted hallways for a little while, stopping only to gaze at a dust-covered photograph that showed a prim-looking family with bright smiles frozen on their faces. The smallest of the family looked to be around the same age as Penelope. After meandering around the musty place for a few more minutes, Penelope started to get bored. There was nothing really creepy about the house other than the fact that it was abandoned. But just as Penelope Park was turning to leave, a door across from her creaked open slightly. Intrigued, she snuck over to it and pulled it open more. Behind the door was an empty room with strange, rust-colored stains on the hardwood floor and peeling wallpaper. Yet what was most interesting was the rhyme that was scratched into the farthest wall.

Wish Kitten, Wish Kitten, grant me a wish, fix all my problems, as quick as a fish.
Wish Kitten, Wish Kitten, I'll do it for you if you just do what I tell you to do.

As soon as Penelope had read the scratching, she felt a weird sensation; as if someone was right behind her, staring. She slowly turned around to find a little tabby kitten with giant cloudy eyes and big ears sitting in front of her. The kitten looked fairly normal, except for his large white eyes, which Penelope assumed was because he was blind. When she knelt down to get a closer look at the creature, he stayed perfectly still except for a blink of his eyes that was so quick it almost seemed as if it hadn't occurred. Penelope had a soft spot for animals of any kind and so she decided that she would take him home. As Penelope marched out of the house holding the kitten in her arms with a smug look on her face, the neighborhood kids cheered and grouped around her in awe. The children were all so amazed that she had made it out unscathed and Penelope was so proud of her accomplishment that none of them realized the kitten was smiling.

The End

Made in the USA
Middletown, DE
09 April 2021